Jill Dow trained at the Royal College of
Art. Since graduating she has worked as a
freelance illustrator specializing in natural
history, including the highly successful
series *Bellamy's Changing World*.
The *Windy Edge Farm* stories are the
first books she has both written
and illustrated.

Jill Dow lives in Thornhill, near Stirling,
Scotland, with her husband and their
young son.

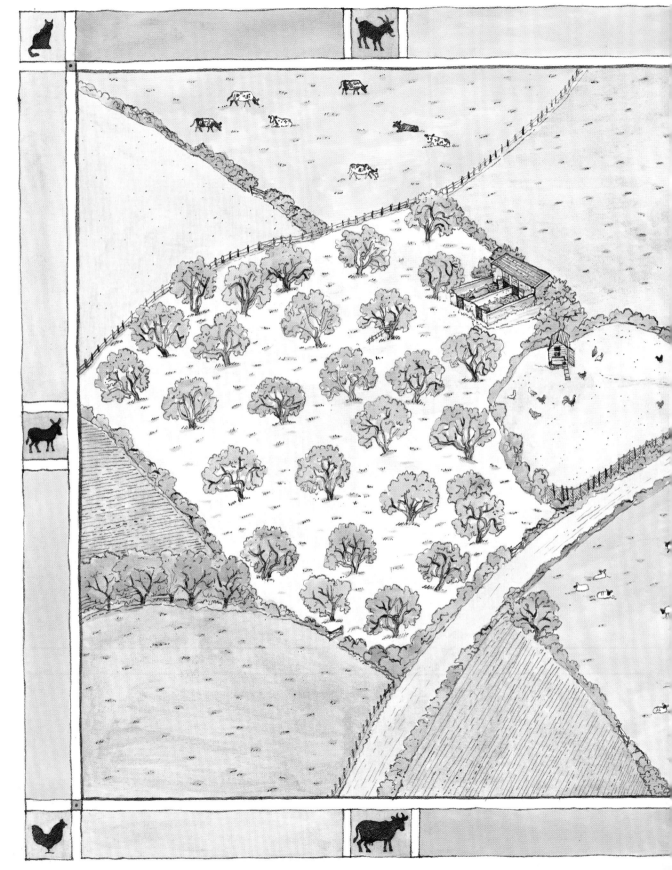

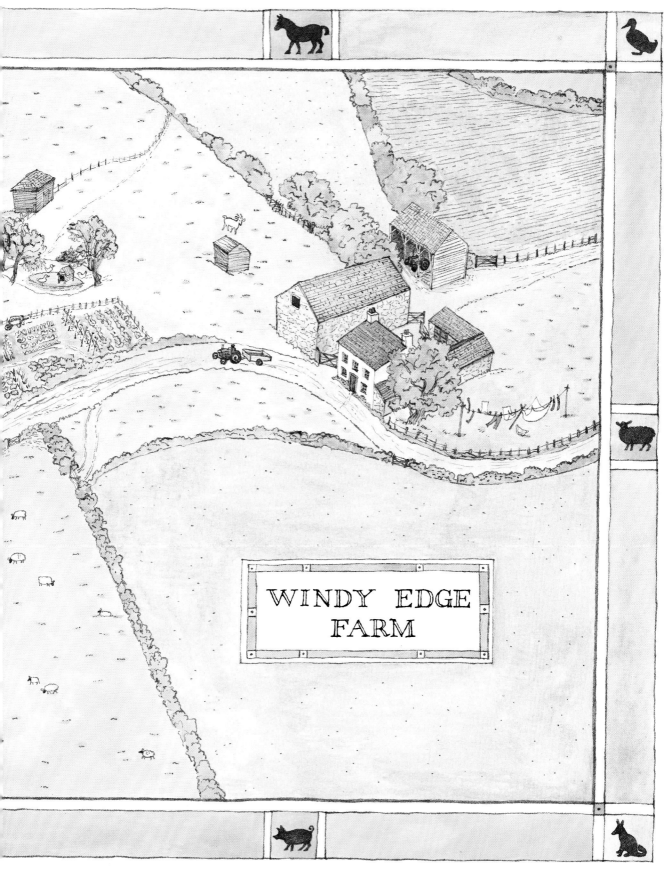

WINDY EDGE
FARM

For Katherine

Text and illustrations copyright © Jill Dow 1990

First published in Great Britain in 1990 by
Frances Lincoln Limited, Apollo Works
5 Charlton Kings Road, London NW5 2SB

British Library Cataloguing in Publication Data
Dow, Jill
    Hepzibah's woolly fleece.
    I. Title   II. Series
    823'.914 [J]

ISBN 0-7112-0615-5 hardback
ISBN 0-7112-0616-3 paperback

Set in Century Schoolbook by Goodfellow & Egan
Printed and bound in Hong Kong

First Frances Lincoln Edition: April 1990

5 7 9 8 6

Design and art direction Debbie MacKinnon

WINDY EDGE FARM

HEPZIBAH'S
WOOLLY FLEECE

Jill Dow

FRANCES LINCOLN

One blustery autumn morning, Mr Finlay turned the sheep into the turnip field to eat up the roots.

Most of the sheep enjoyed having a change from eating grass, but Hepzibah wasn't so sure she liked the taste of turnips. She spotted some tasty grass over by the hedge and off she trotted, across the field.

Her mother called her back, but Hepzibah pretended not to hear.

Hepzibah had eaten only one mouthful of grass when – whoosh – a sudden gust of wind took her by surprise and blew her into the hedge. Her long wool was caught fast on a prickly bramble bush, and the more Hepzibah twisted and tugged, the more tangled she became.

"Baaaaaah! Baaaaaah!" she called to her mother for help. "Baaaaaaaah!" But her bleating was drowned by the noise of the wind, and none of the other sheep could hear her.

Hepzibah felt very sorry for herself. If only her fleece was still as short and springy as it had been when she was a lamb. Then she had jumped and played wherever she liked without getting tangled up in the hedge.

All day long she waited for someone to rescue her, while all around her the spiders were slowly spinning their webs.

At last, when the light was beginning to fade, Mr Finlay and Angus came to check the flock and found poor Hepzibah.

"You silly old sheep!" said Angus, and he stroked her head while his father carefully untangled her wool. "Don't you know to stay away from the brambles?"

Hepzibah certainly did know now.

Soon it was winter, and most of the animals at Windy Edge Farm had to stay inside to keep warm.

The cows huddled together in the barn,

and in the pigsty Samson and Sarah rolled
themselves up in the straw.

But the sheep were left outside, and now
Hepzibah was very glad she had such a long
thick fleece.

It kept her warm and dry all through the short frosty days and long icy nights of winter.

In the spring, when Hepzibah had her own
lamb for the first time, her soft thick wool kept
him warm too. She grew very proud of her
fleece, and was careful never to go too close to
the brambles or the barbed wire fence.

Then came the summer. The growing lambs
ran and played in the sunshine, but Hepzibah
and the other mother sheep would not join in.
They felt hot and uncomfortable inside their
heavy woollen overcoats, and all they could do
was lie in the shade, too tired to move.

Hepzibah's fleece was dusty and scruffy, and
she forgot why she had ever been so proud of it.

Early one morning the flock was woken by
Jess and Ruff the sheepdogs. They ran round,
barking and nipping with their teeth until
every sheep was on its feet.

The sleepy sheep grumbled as the dogs drove
them through the orchard towards the
sheepfold. Hepzibah was very angry at being
made to run about so early in the morning.

Guided by the dogs, the sheep jostled into the sheepfold, and Angus closed the gate behind them. Hepzibah wondered what was going to happen, but there was no time to worry.

"You're first, Hepzibah," said Mr Finlay. He caught hold of her and pulled her out of the pen.

Then he turned Hepzibah
onto her back, and started
up the electric clippers.
Hepzibah began to struggle.
   "Hold still, Hepzibah,"
shouted Mr Finlay,
"it's all for your own good."
And he sliced into
her wool.

Mr Finlay was a very
skilful shearer. With
quick and careful
strokes he clipped the
fleece away from
Hepzibah's body,
without once cutting
her skin.

The whole fleece peeled off in one piece, leaving a smaller, cleaner, whiter and COOLER Hepzibah underneath.

What a relief! Hepzibah skipped and jumped like a lamb. It felt so good to be rid of that heavy woollen overcoat.

"I suppose I can always grow another one," she thought.

And in the autumn, that's just what
Hepzibah did!

– The End –